The DARKSIDE

A TALE OF FAMILY, JUSTICE AND REVENGE

BY
SAMARIA BROWN

Table of Contents

CHAPTER ONE

The Whispering Moonlight

As Luna poured out her heart, the weight of the truth began to lift, replaced by a glimmer of hope. Her mother's words of love and support wrapped around her like a warm blanket, providing a sanctuary amidst the storm. Together, they vowed to face the darkness that had invaded their lives, to protect one another from its chilling grasp.

Days turned into weeks, and Luna found solace not only within the walls of her home but also within the arms of friends who had become like family. They surrounded her with their unwavering support, a shield against the harsh realities that seemed to lurk around every corner. Their laughter and kind words became a balm for her wounded soul, slowly healing the scars left behind by the haunting revelations.

Luna, now armed with strength and determination, embarked on a journey of resilience and self-discovery. The once bleak canvas of fear and uncertainty began to transform into a vibrant tapestry of courage and hope. She grew to understand that the chilling events of her past did not define her, but rather shaped her into the resilient and compassionate person she had become.

As Luna walked through life, she carried the weight of her secrets with grace and resilience. They no longer crushed her, but rather propelled her forward. She became an advocate for those who had suffered in silence, a voice for those who had been silenced. Luna's journey became a beacon of light for others who had felt trapped by their own secrets, inspiring them to find the strength to break free from the suffocating prison of silence.

Through Luna's story, the power of truth and the healing that can come from sharing one's pain became evident. The tendrils of dawn that once cast long shadows across her tear-streaked face now illuminated a path of hope and triumph. With each passing day, Luna continued to embrace her newfound freedom, realizing that her journey was far from over.

She had faced the darkest depths of her own soul and emerged stronger than ever before. Luna had learned that the treacherous enemy of sleep and the haunting events of her past could not overpower the resilience and love that resided within her. With her head held high, Luna stepped forward into a future filled with endless possibilities, armed with the knowledge that she had the strength to overcome any darkness that may come her way.

With unwavering determination, Luna's mother confronted her husband, refusing to continue living under the facade of normalcy that he had meticulously constructed over years of deception. As the truth was revealed, the once familiar walls of their home echoed with the sounds of accusations being hurled like daggers and tears flowing like rivers. It was a heartbreaking scene, a family torn apart by the devastating revelations.

The authorities were notified, and their involvement set in motion a chain of events that would forever change the course of Luna's life. The legal process was a daunting labyrinth of bureaucracy and emotional turmoil that demanded immense courage and resilience. Luna had to relive the trauma in excruciating detail, her voice trembling with fear and anger as she confronted her father in the sterile confines of the courtroom.

The trial itself became a grueling ordeal, a constant reminder of the violation she had endured. Luna fought through every painful testimony, determined to seek justice and put an end to the suffering. Though the courtroom was a symbol of her pain, she held onto a glimmer of hope that flickered within her, guiding her through the darkness.

Finally, after what seemed like an eternity, the verdict was reached. Luna felt a wave of relief and validation wash over her as the truth was acknowledged, and her father held accountable for his actions. It was a small victory, yet it meant so much more to Luna. However, she knew that this was not the end of her journey.

The scars of the trauma remained, etched deep within her soul. Luna had battled her demons in the courtroom, but the healing process was just beginning. With therapy, support from loved ones, and sheer determination, Luna embarked on a journey of healing and self-discovery. It was a process that would test her strength, but she was determined to reclaim her life and rebuild from the ruins left behind. With each passing day, Luna showed resilience and a remarkable ability to rise above the darkness, slowly but steadily healing the wounds inflicted upon her.

Though her journey was far from over, Luna had come a long way from the shattered fragments of her past. She had found strength in confronting her fears, seeking justice, and ultimately refusing to let her father's actions define her. Luna was a survivor, determined to create a future that was free from the pain and cruelty she had endured. And with each step forward, she gained not only her own freedom but also served as an inspiration to others facing similar battles.

As Luna stepped out of the courtroom, the sun's warm glow illuminated her triumphant smile, symbolizing the start of a new chapter in her life. The path that lay ahead stretched out before her, intimidating and filled with uncertainty. It was a journey that promised to be full of challenges and obstacles, but Luna was no longer alone in this struggle. Throughout her harrowing experiences, she had found her voice, a resilient force that could never be silenced.

With each confident step she took, Luna left behind the haunting shadows of her past, moving forward with a renewed sense of hope and the promise of healing. The bruises and scars may have healed on the surface, but the emotional wounds she carried would take time to fully mend. However, Luna was determined. She had transformed from a timid girl living in constant fear to a brave soul ready to face the world head-on. Her newfound courage, matched with her unwavering determination, allowed her to reclaim the light that had been cruelly stolen from her.

Yet, the shadows of her past still loomed at the edges of her vision, a constant reminder of the darkness she had overcome. They awaited their chance to once again engulf her in their suffocating grasp. The fight for justice and healing was far from over, and Luna was well aware that it would be a long and grueling battle. But she refused to succumb to their presence. She was no longer the naive child who had once been completely consumed by their darkness. Luna had emerged from the depths as a survivor, a warrior with an unyielding spirit. She vowed to continue her fight until the light had finally vanquished the shadows, and her journey towards complete liberation was realized.

CHAPTER TWO

A New Beginning

The suburban house stood proudly on the avenue, its exterior glowing in the warm hues that only the nighttime sun could bestow. It was a sight that beckoned to anyone who passed by, a beacon of desire in a sea of ordinary homes. Luna, clutching Smile tightly in her arms, took a step across the threshold and entered a world that seemed to vibrate with endless possibilities. As the door closed behind them, it almost whispered promises of safety and security, wrapping Luna in a comforting cocoon. In that moment, Luna found herself sandwiched between the harsh reality of her past and the tantalizing potential of this new beginning.

Just as Luna's heart began to soar with a newfound hope, Chanel, Luna's cousin, appeared like a guardian angel emerging from the shadows of the hallway. In her eyes, Luna saw a reflection of her own journey — a tale etched with hardship and resilience. Their embrace was not simply familial; it was a fusion of two narratives, two souls intertwined by their shared experiences. Luna couldn't help but feel like she was stepping into the pages of a fairy tale, where she was the modern-day Cinderella finding solace and support in the kinship of her fairy godmother.

The room that had been assigned to Luna and Smile seemed to unfold like a scene from a storybook. Soft, soothing shades of lavender and powder blue covered the walls, casting a calming aura over the space. The air held a hint of magic, as if the room itself had been enchanted. Whimsical mobiles twirled above the crib, their delicate movements casting playful shadows that seemed to come alive, almost like characters in a fanciful play. Gently, Luna placed Smile in the crib, feeling as though she was orchestrating the prologue of a tale that was yet to be written.

As the night settled around them, the house became a beacon of warmth and life. It was as if the walls and floors were infused with the enchanting melodies of an imaginary utopia. The air was filled with the tantalizing aroma of Chanel's culinary wizardry, her dishes transcended the boundaries of mere sustenance, luring anyone who entered the kitchen into a realm of alchemy. Luna, entranced by the sight before her, couldn't help but feel as if she had stepped into a fairytale, where every ingredient held the power to heal and nourish not only the body but also the soul.

The kitchen table, transformed into a sacred space, served as a round table of fellowship where Luna, Chanel, and Smile gathered. Each plate presented a culinary delight, carefully crafted with love and resilience, becoming artifacts in a museum of triumph. Luna found herself marveling at the symbolism embedded within each dish, realizing that they were not only a feast for the senses but also a celebration of their journey towards overcoming adversity. As they sat together, Luna sensed a surge of strength within her, feeling like the protagonist embarking on a heroic adventure, surrounded by allies who had willingly joined her on her quest for inner restoration.

Chanel, whose expertise extended beyond the realm of culinary arts, became Luna's mentor in the intricate dance of motherhood. In this enchanted haven, the lullabies she sang weren't just melodious tunes but powerful incantations, capable of weaving spells of comfort and tranquility around Luna and her child. And in the midst of it all, Smile's laughter rang out like the joyful chimes of mischievous fairy sprites, creating an atmosphere of pure magic that reverberated throughout the entire house. It was a gentle reminder that magic dwelled not only in the most obvious and expected places but also in the unexpected and mundane, bringing joy and wonder to everyday life.

Beyond the partitions of their imaginary sanctuary, the neighborhood spread out like a tapestry of interconnected stories. Each neighbor became a character in

Luna's narrative, offering each imaginary and real support. The streets, with their captivating cobblestones, echoed with the footsteps of newfound pals who appeared to step out of the pages of Luna's fairy tale.

In her journey through her imagined haven, Luna's mind was immersed in a remarkable odyssey of self-discovery. The scars carved deep into her psyche were no longer mere reminders of the painful battles she had fought, but had transformed into mystical symbols that held profound meaning. They served as constant companions, reminding her of the strength she had harnessed in times of turmoil. With each passing day, Luna realized that healing was not simply about escaping the clutches of darkness, but rather about embracing both the light and the shadows, finding harmony in the dissonance of her existence.

As the moon hung low in the night sky, Luna stood at the precipice of an uncertain future. The allure of her imaginary utopia did not fully alleviate the nagging doubts that simmered within her, like whispers carried by the wind. Was this newfound sanctuary truly a safe haven, or was it merely a temporary respite? Luna, much like a protagonist in the midst of her own story, contemplated the enigmatic mysteries that lay ahead, fully aware that the forthcoming chapters of her life were yet unwritten.

Seeking Justice

Within the haven of Chanel's home, Luna found solace and strength amidst the chaos that her father's actions had caused. The warmth and love within her cousin's living room seemed to provide a shield against the painful memories that lingered in the shadows. As Luna navigated through the unfamiliar territory of seeking justice, she couldn't help but reflect on how these suburban streets, once mere backdrops to her refuge, now bore witness to her tentative steps towards empowerment.

In the cozy kitchen, sipping chamomile tea, Chanel and Luna discussed the gravity of the path they were embarking on. Chanel, a guiding light of knowledge and support, explained the intricacies of reporting such heinous acts and the daunting prison process that lay ahead. Each sip of tea seemed to infuse Luna with a newfound courage and determination.

The decision to file charges against her own father was not simply a legal step, but a declaration of Luna's strength and resilience. The imaginary veil of protection that she had spun around herself for so long was now taking on a tangible form as she dialed the local authorities. The conversation hung heavy with the weight of reality, as Luna spoke the unspeakable truths, unraveling the narrative that had held her captive for far too long.

With Chanel's silent encouragement, Luna found her voice, laying bare the painful history that had kept her silent and imprisoned. It was a moment of both vulnerability and triumph, as Luna took the first step towards reclaiming her own life and seeking the justice she so rightly deserved. From this point on, Luna's journey would be defined by her strength, resilience, and unwavering determination to confront the darkness and find healing in the light.

The subsequent days had been an intense whirlwind of emotions and experiences for Luna. It was a tempest of prison procedures and emotional reckonings that she had to face head-on. She was observed and supported by Chanel, who stood by her side throughout the daunting task of recounting her traumatic experiences to strangers. These strangers were police officers, who listened with stoic expressions but diligently jotted down the painful chapters of Luna's life. It was not just a simple journey through the legal labyrinth in search of justice; it was an odyssey of confronting her demons and a cathartic exercise that left Luna emotionally drained but strangely liberated.

The courtroom, with its austere atmosphere, became the stage where Luna's truth was put under intense scrutiny. The prosecutor skillfully painted a vivid picture of Luna's harrowing experiences, wielding words like powerful weapons against her father's denial. Seated on the witness stand, Luna could feel the weight of the courtroom audience's gaze upon her. It was a collective gaze that seemed to dissect her pain, searching for any signs of inconsistency. On the other hand, the defense took a predictable approach, attempting to cast doubt on Luna's credibility and relegate her truth to the realm of imagination.

However, amidst this gripping chapter of legal drama, Luna discovered strength in unexpected places. The prosecutor, a figure of justice personified, became her ally and a formidable warrior who fought with the law as a shield to protect Luna from her tormentor. The courtroom, resembling a battlefield of words, witnessed Luna stand tall in the face of adversity. As she bravely recounted her experiences, the walls seemed to reverberate with collective gasps of attention—a shared acknowledgment that although justice may be elusive, it was worth pursuing.

As Luna emerged from the courtroom, a wave of relief washed over her. The guilty verdict she had yearned for had finally been delivered. The weight of injustice that had burdened her for so long lifted, allowing a flicker of hope to reignite within her. However, as she stepped out into the world beyond those courtroom walls, Luna found herself confronted with a array of conflicting emotions.

The victory in court did little to heal the deep wounds that had been carved into her soul. The scars of the past remained, their presence a constant reminder of the pain she had endured. While justice had been served, Luna realized that closure was not as simple as a single courtroom decision. She found herself at a crossroads, facing the choice between moving forward and embracing the unexpected challenges that lay ahead, or dwelling in the shadows of her past.

In the embrace of her newfound haven, Luna experienced a paradox. The triumph of justice did not immediately absolve her of the nightmares that continued to haunt her nights. The echoes of the courtroom merged with the specters of her past, creating a labyrinth of emotions that she had to navigate through. Closure seemed elusive, for the battle had not only been fought in the courtroom, but within the depths of her own mind as well.

As Luna took a deep breath and closed her eyes, she knew that her journey was far from over. The quest for justice had been won, but the healing of her spirit required a different kind of battle. She would need to confront the demons that still lingered within, to face the darkness head-on, and to find a way to move forward. The road ahead was uncertain, but Luna was filled with a newfound strength and determination. She would not allow her past to define her future, nor would she let the echoes of the courtroom drown out the whispers of her own resilience. With each step towards healing, Luna's path began to unfold, guiding her towards a new chapter in her life—one marked not only by the pursuit of justice, but by the pursuit of her own inner peace.

As Luna stood on the quiet street, basking in the soft light emitted by the streetlights outside Chanel's house, she couldn't help but reflect on the start of her journey. It felt like just yesterday when she had found the courage to take that first step towards recovery. However, she knew that this was just the beginning. There were still many chapters to be written in her story, with uncertain horizons lurking beyond the steps of the courthouse.

The taste of justice was still fresh in Luna's mind. It was a hard-fought victory, one that held great significance for her. It served as a powerful punctuation mark in the evolving narrative of her resilience. This triumphant moment was a poignant reminder that despite the numerous challenges she had faced, the pursuit of restoration had the ability to bring about a brand new dawn.

As Luna continued to stand outside Chanel's home, she couldn't help but feel a renewed sense of hope and determination. The road to recovery was long and arduous, filled with obstacles she never thought she could overcome. Yet, here she was, stronger than ever, ready to continue writing her story with bravery and resilience.

The promise of a brighter future propelled Luna forward. She knew the path ahead would be filled with its fair share of hardships and uncertainties, but she was no longer afraid. The support she had received from those who believed in her, the strength she had discovered within herself, all fueled her determination to persevere.

With each step she took, Luna embraced the journey ahead with open arms, knowing that it would ultimately lead her to a place of healing and growth. The shadows of her past would slowly fade away, replaced by the warmth of the sun's first rays. And with every sunrise, Luna's spirit would be reawakened, ready to face whatever challenges lay ahead, and eager to create a future filled with joy and fulfillment.

CHAPTER FOUR

The Trial

In the courtroom, it was as though a battleground had been erected, a space where Luna's reality clashed with her father's unwavering denial. The prosecution, equipped with Luna's harrowing narrative, meticulously constructed a vivid depiction of her protracted suffering, like an artist carefully painting vibrant strokes that revealed the unimaginable brutality she had endured. Each word spoken by the prosecution seemed to reverberate through the hallowed court, echoing like a mournful tolling bell, casting a stark and haunting contrast to her father's desperate and futile attempts to deflect any sense of guilt or responsibility. It was a gripping and gut-wrenching spectacle, as the truth unfolded before the court's eyes and the weight of justice hung heavily in the air.

Seated at the witness stand, Luna could feel the intense gaze of the court upon her. It felt as though she was being examined by a silent and discerning tribunal, one that was not only scrutinizing her testimony but also dissecting the very core of her pain. The defense, resembling shadowy adversaries, left no stone unturned in their efforts to tarnish Luna's credibility, attempting to dismiss her truth as nothing more than a figment of a tormented imagination. However, amidst this intimidating and unforgiving legal arena, Luna found an unexpected and unwavering ally in the prosecutor. Like a stalwart and protective guardian, the prosecutor stood beside her, fortified her against the relentless onslaught of doubt and skepticism.

The courtroom drama unfolded with a tumultuous cadence, each day marked by a turbulent wave of emotions. Luna, flanked by her steadfast cousin and bolstered by the unwavering commitment of the prosecutor, stood as an indomitable force. Every question hurled at her, every answer she gave, became a veritable battlefield where Luna's courage clashed head-on with the vehement denial of her father. The air inside the courtroom crackled with tension, the atmosphere heavy with the unspoken horrors that had brought Luna to this moment. As the trial continued, the weight of Luna's pain and the quest for justice hung palpably in the air, creating a sense of anticipation and unease among everyone present.

As the trial progressed, Luna found herself on an emotional journey, confronting her own father in a face-to-face encounter that left her shaken to her core. The intensity of the moment was overwhelming, as Luna held her father's gaze and saw a mix of defiance and guilt in his eyes. The courtroom itself became a crucible of emotions, with Luna's unwavering resilience standing in stark contrast to her father's desperate attempts to evade responsibility.

Days turned into weeks, and the trial reached its highest point, the moment of reckoning that had been building up. The atmosphere in the courtroom was charged with anticipation, as everyone held their breath, waiting for the monumental verdict to be delivered. The weight of the years of torment that Luna had endured, the hope for justice, and the fear of disappointment, all merged together in that crucial moment.

And then, with a resounding thud, the judge's gavel fell, pronouncing the guilty verdict. The impact of those words hit Luna like an unrelenting tidal wave, crashing over her and leaving her reeling. Relief and sorrow intertwined within her, creating a tempest of conflicting emotions that refused to be neatly categorized.

Stepping out of the courtroom, Luna couldn't shake the heavy burden that the guilty verdict had placed upon her. It clung to her like an indelible shroud, a symbolic triumph of justice tainted by the haunting shadows of a painful past.

As Luna stood at the precipice of closure and uncertainty, she couldn't help but feel overwhelmed. The trial had been a grueling and emotionally draining experience, but it had also brought a sense of justice and finality. However, the scars that had been etched into her soul would not simply fade away with the verdict. The criminal's triumph marked the end of one harrowing chapter in her life, but she knew that the journey towards healing and recovery was far from over.

As the doors of the courtroom closed behind her with a resounding thud, Luna was faced with the daunting task of moving forward. The echoes of her testimony were still fresh in her mind, as were the reactions of the spectators who had been riveted by the trial. The collective gasps, sighs, and stifled tears lingered in the air, a poignant reminder of the emotions that had coursed through the courtroom.

Stepping beyond the courthouse steps, Luna was confronted with the unknown horizons that lay before her. The path ahead promised to be filled with unexpected challenges and obstacles, yet there was a glimmer of hope that accompanied her. It was a flickering and fragile flame, but it was enough to guide her through the darkness that still loomed over her.

The trial had been a visceral and emotionally charged experience, one that had tested Luna's courage and resolve. It had forced her to confront the darkest corners of her past, the scars that had shaped her into the person she was today. And now, as the chapter came to a close, Luna knew that she would need to draw upon that same fierce determination in order to navigate the aftermath.

Recovery was not a destination but a lifelong odyssey, one that would require strength, resilience, and a relentless pursuit of healing. Luna had come to accept that her scarred past would always be a part of her, but she was determined not to let it define her. With every step she took, Luna knew that she was rewriting her story, forging a new path towards a future that held the promise of wholeness and peace.

CHAPTER FIVE

The Verdict

In the midst of the once-charged court docket's eerily still atmosphere, Luna found herself on the precipice of a new reality. It was a paradoxical moment, characterized by a mixture of relief and trepidation. The sound of the resounding gavel declaring her father guilty still echoed in her mind, although the path to justice had proven to be a bewildering journey filled with unexpected turns.

Stepping outside into the cold embrace of truth, Luna couldn't shake off the weight of the guilty verdict. It was a bittersweet triumph, entangled with threads of depression. The legal system had acknowledged her pain, yet the scars etched into her soul remained. The verdict, much like a double-edged sword, held the promise of vindication, but it also signified the daunting path she had yet to face in the aftermath of the trial.

Hungry for sensational narratives, the media converged outside the courthouse like vultures anticipating their prey. Luna, with the protection of her cousin and the prosecutor, bravely walked through a gauntlet of flashing cameras and probing microphones. The onslaught of prying questions aimed not only to dissect the details of the trial but to unravel the very essence of Luna's resilience. Her silence became her strongest shield—an unwavering response to a world eager to exploit her vulnerability.

In the aftermath of the trial, Luna found herself caught in a whirlwind of conflicting emotions and thoughts. The guilty verdict, a vindication of the horrific experiences she had endured, clashed with the realization that justice, though served, could not erase the deep-seated pain caused by her father's actions. The wounds she carried, invisible to the naked eye, reminded her of the trauma of a past that could not be contained within the boundaries of a courtroom.

Luna rode on a rollercoaster of emotions, a mix of relief, sorrow, and an intense focus that made it clear the conflict was far from over. An unexpected companion, guilt, took root in the deepest corners of her mind. The judgment of society, not limited to the courtroom, weighed heavily upon her, analyzing not just her father's crimes but also scrutinizing her perceived role in the unfolding drama.

The days that followed the verdict were like a surreal blur for Luna. She navigated through a world that alternated between sympathetic nods and suspicious glances, grappling with the aftermath of the trial. Although the legal system had been a steadfast ally, it proved incapable of healing the shattered fragments of her soul. The guilty verdict, though a testament to her truth, could not shield her from the haunting shadows that lingered in the corners of her consciousness.

The chapter in Luna's life began with her facing the complexities of life after the trial. While the guilty verdict brought a sense of closure, she quickly realized that her journey was far from over. Looking ahead, Luna saw an unpredictable road filled with the wreckage of shattered beliefs and a broken family. The post-trial existence seemed like a labyrinth, and Luna faced the daunting task of not only rebuilding her life, but also rediscovering her identity. The guilty verdict had a profound impact, not just for Luna, but for society as a whole. Its powerful message resonated like a wake-up call, forcing people to reflect on their ingrained perceptions and confront the hidden epidemic of abuse that silently plagued many lives.

As Luna navigated through the aftermath, the chapter came to a close with a bittersweet realization: the guilty verdict was not the end, but merely a significant marker on her path towards healing. The journey towards recovery was full of uncertainty, but it also held the promise of self-discovery. The echoes of the trial continued to haunt Luna's soul like a haunting melody, shaping not just her present, but also the unwritten chapters of her future.

CHAPTER SIX

The Threat

The aftermath of Luna's tumultuous trial sent shockwaves through her life, leaving her caught in a paradoxical blend of conflicting emotions. As the courtroom proccedings came to an end, Luna felt a temporary relief, as if the weight of her past traumas had been momentarily lifted. It was as if she could finally see a glimmer of hope and a chance for a fresh start. Little did she know, however, that her journey was far from over.

The first sign of trouble came in the form of a phone call, a seemingly harmless interruption in her newfound peace. The caller ID displayed an unfamiliar number, foreshadowing the storm that was about to descend upon her. With trembling hands, Luna answered the call, her voice laced with the remnants of her past apprehension.

"Hello?" she cautiously greeted, already sensing that this conversation would unravel her fragile sense of security. The response on the other end was an unsettling silence, a pause that seemed to stretch on for an eternity. Then, like a venomous serpent revealing itself, Luna's father's voice slithered through the receiver, sending a cold shiver down her spine.

In that moment, Luna realized that her father's presence was an unexpected and unwelcome reminder of the fear and anxiety she thought she had left behind. The remnants of her harrowing journey were still present, manifesting in this unexpected phone call that threatened to drag her back into the clutches of her deepest fears. As her father's sinister voice echoed in her ears, Luna couldn't help but wonder how she would navigate this new chapter of her life and whether she would ever truly find peace.

The chilling words of Luna's father, filled with malice and threat, resonated through the airwaves and seeped into the sanctuary of her cousin's home. The prison, once seen as a symbol of justice, now served as a channel for her father's malevolence, amplifying the fear and despair that consumed her. The vile threats that emanated from her smartphone were a grotesque reminder that even the guilty verdict couldn't extinguish the flames of her familial torment.

Living within the supposed safety of her cousin's home, Luna felt a creeping sense of fear encroaching upon her newfound sanctuary. The danger, intangible and elusive, loomed like a shadowy specter, eclipsing the fragile light at the end of Luna's tunnel. The flawed fortress of the legal system appeared pitifully inadequate in protecting her from the insidious threat that now infiltrated every aspect of her existence.

Driven by desperation and a deep-rooted fear of regression, Luna found herself at a pivotal crossroads. The long-rejected notion of seeking revenge began to take root in the fertile soil of her pain, blossoming into a dangerous flower with petals of retribution. The plan, conceived in the crucible of her darkest impulses, unfolded like a surreal odyssey: a treacherous journey into the depths of Luna's vengeful resolve.

Her cousin, a steadfast ally navigating the turbulent seas of Luna's tribulations, found herself torn between the conflicting instincts of caution and empathy. On one hand, she felt the need to warn Luna about the dangers that lay ahead, to shield her from further suffering. Yet, on the other hand, there was a deep understanding of Luna's desperate plea for relief, a desire to alleviate her pain. It was within the secrecy of their clandestine conversations that a plan began to take shape—a plan that resembled a forbidden dance with the unknown future. It was a perilous gambit, one that danced dangerously close to the edge of moral ambiguity. The line between right and wrong, so clearly defined before, now appeared as nothing more than a nebulous haze.

And so, the chapter started with Luna and her cousin embarking upon a treacherous journey of vengeance.

The plan, born in the depths of despair, unfolded like an intricate tapestry of manipulation. Each thread carefully woven, each decision made with the weight of moral compromise. Luna remained oblivious to the consequences that lay in wait, lurking in the shadows. Unbeknownst to her, her quest for retribution hung precariously by a delicate thread, ready to unravel at any moment.

As the chapter reached its climax, Luna found herself standing at the precipice of her darkest impulses and the harrowing truth of her actions. The risks, once confined to prison cells, now permeated the very air she breathed. Her pursuit of justice had transformed into a dangerous dance with the shadows. The specter of revenge loomed over her every move, casting a long and ominous shadow over her fragile sense of normalcy. Readers were left on the edge of their seats, yearning to know the fateful consequences that awaited Luna in the upcoming chapters, eager for resolution to the growing tension that had built with each turn of the page.

CHAPTER SEVEN

The Plan

In the dimly lit chamber, the room seemed to come alive with an eerie glow, casting long shadows that danced and swirled around Luna and Chanel, who stood huddled together like conspirators in a forbidden masquerade. Their presence filled the air, thickening it with anticipation, as if they were about to embark on something truly extraordinary.

Luna, with an air of mystery surrounding her, took center stage as she began to unfold her plan for revenge. Each word she spoke held a weight that reverberated through the room, every heartbeat echoing in harmony with the secrets she unveiled. It was as though the very walls themselves had become witnesses to their clandestine plot, their presence immortalized in the spectral residue that adorned their surroundings.

As Luna delved deeper into the intricate details of her plan, the room transformed into a theater of shadows. Whispers of vengeance fluttered around them, their ghostly presence leaving invisible marks in the tapestry of their destinies. Chanel, feeling the powerful pull of Luna's conviction, found herself drawn into a dance with the unknown, teetering on the edge of morality.

Within this sanctuary of intrigue, the room seemed to exhale an atmosphere heavy with secrecy. The scent of it hung in the air, intoxicating and thrilling, as Luna's radiant eyes flickered like two incandescent stars in the darkness. The suspense, palpable and alive, coiled around them, infusing every clandestine revelation with heightened stakes.

In this moment, it was clear that their plan had taken on a life of its own. It was no longer just a collection of events, but a narrative that transcended the ordinary. Luna's ambition, bold and audacious, fueled their every move, as they embarked on a journey where the boundaries of right and wrong began to blur.

In the elaborate game of high-stakes chess, their cousin found themselves unknowingly caught in the middle, becoming the focus of Luna's grand scheme. Like ethereal messengers, encrypted messages traveled between the conspirators, leaving behind enigmatic breadcrumbs for others to follow. The room, a silent witness to their treacherous plot, absorbed these missives, its walls echoing with the resonance of their secretive plans.

Each night unfolded like a surreptitious ballet, drawing Luna and Chanel further into the depths of their dangerous alliance. Cryptic symbols and coded language floated through the air, creating an atmosphere that seemed to transcend the boundaries of the mundane. The suspense in the room grew, a palpable pressure that slithered like a serpentine waltz, leaving no corner untouched. The walls, adorned with the shadows of their whispered confessions, bore witness to the birth of a plan that brazenly defied moral boundaries.

Luna's thirst for revenge echoed throughout the room, a dark sonata composed of desperation and unwavering determination. As Luna and Chanel embarked on this perilous adventure, the room transformed into a crucible of emotions. Fear and anticipation intermingled, charging the air with an electric intensity. The plan itself seemed to take on a life of its own, a living organism that breathed with a cadence only understood by those who dared to challenge the very concept of justice.

The room, still throbbing with the echoes of their clandestine percent, held inside its partitions the unspoken covenant among Luna and Chanel

CHAPTER EIGHT

Unveiling Shadows

In the aftermath of Luna's audacious plan, the room underwent a breathtaking metamorphosis. Shadows, like a symphony of darkness, danced across the walls, seemingly alive and guided by unseen forces. Luna and Chanel, at the center of this enigmatic ballet, found themselves entangled in a dance of consequences.

As Luna surveyed the room, she felt as though the shadows held whispered secrets that only they could comprehend. Chanel, once a confidante and now a co-

conspirator, stood beside Luna, their connection intertwined with the newfound power coursing through the room. The walls, bearing the weight of their shared secret, seemed to pulsate with an otherworldly resonance.

Days blurred into nights, and Luna traversed the maze of her emotions. The room, now a sacred sanctuary, echoed with the weight of her regret. Luna's path to redemption, fragile and delicate, shimmered with each hesitant step towards self-forgiveness.

Suspense hung heavy in the air, a tangible force that defied the laws of physics. Luna and Chanel moved through the aftermath like actors on a surreal stage. The shadows, no longer mere absence of light, danced in harmony with the pair, casting an ethereal glow upon their transformation. Closure, once a distant star, now beckoned like a cosmic riddle within the room's celestial symphony.

The room in which Luna found herself was a sight to behold, a celestial canvas for introspection. It seemed to emanate an otherworldly energy, vibrating with the cosmic hum of Luna's inner war. As Luna sat in contemplation, each paragraph she wrote opened up like a star being born, each word revealing the intricate details of her ongoing battle. The depth of her thoughts and emotions painted a vivid picture in the minds of those who read her words. And yet, despite the tumultuous nature of Luna's journey, there was a sense of closure that shimmered within the room. Like a celestial frame, it encapsulated Luna's consciousness, keeping her thoughts and experiences orbiting in a constant, mesmerizing dance. As readers embarked on this cosmic ballet of revelation, they too were suspended within the room, captivated by the sheer magnitude of Luna's story.

CHAPTER NINE

Embracing Shadows

In the aftermath's cosmic haven, Luna and Chanel found themselves transformed into celestial beings, their auras intertwined with the nebulous aftermath swirling around them. Shadows, once mundane and ordinary, had now taken on a cosmic form, pulsating with an otherworldly energy that infused their surroundings. The room itself seemed to come alive with strokes from a cosmic palette, as if the very essence of the universe was being painted onto its walls.

Luna and Chanel, now cosmic voyagers, stood at the precipice of a daunting task - the cosmic project of closure. Each night became a cosmic adventure in self-reflection for Luna, as she gazed into the vast cosmic expanse, searching for answers and solutions to the cosmic mysteries that surrounded her. Chanel, a steadfast companion on this cosmic odyssey, felt the gravitational pull of their shared secret weighing heavily on her soul. The very walls of the room they found themselves in seemed to mirror their cosmic journey, warping and bending with the cosmic energies of Luna's transformation.

As Luna and Chanel continued to tread through the intricate pathways of their cosmic labyrinth of emotions, the room itself seemed to transform into a cosmic vessel. It became a conduit for the ebb and flow of remorse, a vessel through which the cosmic forces of closure coursed through. Closure, a cosmic enigma in its own right, danced on the event horizon of Luna's consciousness, teetering on the edge of her attention. The suspense that hung in the air was like a cosmic melody, guiding readers through the twists and turns of Luna's inner cosmic warfare, as she grappled with the cosmic forces that threatened to consume her.

This cosmic chapter, with its ethereal essence, unfolded gracefully, akin to a gentle cosmic breeze that brushed against the fabric of the universe. In its entirety, each paragraph within this chapter served as a profound cosmic ripple, resonating through the tapestry of Luna's redemption. These words, like celestial echoes, served to underline and accentuate the intricate cosmic complexities that accompanied Luna on her transformative journey.

As the shadows cast by Luna's past actions evolved, they too became cosmic echoes, mere remnants of the cosmic battles she had fought and the choices she had made. Each echo acted as a poignant reminder of her cosmic transformation, contrasting her current state with the turmoil she had once experienced. The interplay of these echoes only served to highlight the profundity of her cosmic voyage.

Yet, amidst it all, closure beckoned Luna, like a celestial destination on her cosmic map. It was not merely a distant, intangible concept, but a cosmic system that held the key to her ultimate redemption. Closure had become the ultimate cosmic frontier in Luna's quest for forgiveness and self-healing. It represented the culmination of her cosmic endeavors, the final piece in the puzzle that would grant her the solace and inner peace she so fervently sought.

In this cosmic narrative, Luna's odyssey towards self-forgiveness unfolded with both breathtaking beauty and cosmic intricacy. Each element, whether it be the cosmic breeze, the shadows turned echoes, or the cosmic system of closure, contributed to the cosmic symphony playing out within Luna's soul. With each passing moment, Luna moved closer to embracing the cosmic redemption she craved, and the cosmic tapestry of her life continued to weave itself into an awe-inspiring and transformative masterpiece.

As Luna stood in the room, feeling the weight of her actions and the consequences they had on her own cosmic journey, she couldn't help but notice a surreal sense of cosmic energy that seemed to linger in the air. It was as if the room itself was resonating with the echoes of her own cosmic choices, amplifying the depth of emotions she had experienced. Each moment, each decision she had made, reverberated through the space, creating an atmospheric tension that pulled readers deeper into Luna's cosmic labyrinth of emotions. It was this suspense, this underlying cosmic force, that guided readers hand in hand with Luna as she navigated the twists and turns of her transformative adventure. And yet, amidst the cosmic turmoil, there was a subtle presence of closure, a cosmic partner that seemed to beckon from the shadows. Though the chapter may have come to an end, the door remained slightly ajar, leaving room for the next cosmic chapter to unfold in Luna's life. With every cosmic turn, the anticipation grew, building an insatiable curiosity for what cosmic wonders awaited Luna on her ongoing cosmic journey of self-discovery.